BEAUTIFUL STRANGER

ALSO BY
KAT VANCIL

THE MARKED ONES TRILOGY

Beautiful Stranger
Daemons in the Mist
The Storm behind Your Eyes
The Other Side of Truth
The Marked Ones: The Complete Trilogy

BRIDE OF THE HARVEST WOLF

Bride of the Harvest Wolf: Episode One
Bride of the Harvest Wolf: Episode Two

THE MARKED ONES TRILOGY
· BOOK 0.5 ·

BEAUTIFUL STRANGER

KAT VANCIL

KORAT PUBLISHING

BEAUTIFUL STRANGER

Copyright © 2014 by Alicia Kat Vancil. All rights reserved.

WWW.KATGIRLSTUDIO.COM

Published by Korat Publishing in California
Printed in the United States of America

This book is a work of fiction. Any references to historical events, real people, or real locales are used fictitiously. Other names, characters, places, and incidents are the products of the author's imagination, and any resemblance to actual events or locales or persons, living or dead, is entirely coincidental.

ISBN: 978-1-937288-06-8 (paperback)
Kindle ASIN: B00KFRR51K

Book design by Alicia Kat Vancil
Cover illustration © 2014 Alicia Kat Vancil
Cover photograph © Piotr Marcinski - Fotolia.com
Cover photograph © anjudan - Fotolia.com

The text for this book is set in Bookerly and Optimus Princeps Semibold

First Edition

*For anyone who has ever dared
to dream that impossible dream.*

Pronunciation Guide

Aku *ah-coo*
Arius *are-ee-us*
Chan *shawn*
Citrina *si-tree-nah*
Daemon *day-mon*
Daemotic *day-mah-tic*
Daenara *day-nar-ah*
Galathea *gala-thee-ah*
Karalia *car-ah-lee-ah*
Kekkoshi sadara *key-koh-she sah-dar-ah*
Mai *my*
Makara *mah-car-ah*
Neodaemon *knee-oh-day-mon*
Nikkalla *nick-a-lah*
Nualla *new-all-ah*
Parakalo *par-ah-kay-low*
Tammore *ta-more*
Vona *voh-nah*

S*URE, WHY NOT. W*HAT HAVE *we got to lose?* is probably the understatement of the year as far as last words go. So why, in the name of all reason, did I say yes? I'm still not one-hundred percent sure, but maybe it was because Nualla was beyond tempting, and I was dying to know her secrets. Or that I was angry with my parents for never being there, and I wanted someone to be close to me. Or that I was really, really drunk. But it was probably because, when fate throws you the one thing you have always wanted, you grab hold of it and never let go.

And even though it's dangerous, and even if I have to leave everything behind, my answer is, and always will be…

Yes.

I Am So Getting Expelled for This

Monday, January 9th

PATRICK

'M TELLING YOU MAN—NEVER gonna happen," Connor said with a snort as he folded his arms and leaned against the locker next to mine. His hair was a surprisingly well-kept spray of dreads pulled neatly into a ponytail. Which meant his mom had probably gotten on his case again and threatened to cut it off if he didn't keep it neat. And knowing Connor, that would probably last for all of a few weeks before it started getting into disarray again.

"Yeah, I know," I sighed as I popped my locker

open. After nearly four years here, I really didn't have to look too hard to spin the dial to the correct combination.

The thing was, I knew it was impossible—me and her—because I would never, in any universe, end up with someone like Nualla Galathea. Because Nualla was...well she didn't look like she should have existed in the real world. Not with wave after wave of jet black, spiraling curls spilling past her hips, and a shock of lapis blue that set off the unusual color of her eyes in a way that was beyond distracting. Really, every time I saw her it felt like someone had dug deep into my mind and crafted her from my dreams. And everything from her heart-shaped face to her dancer's body that filled out her Bayside Academy uniform in all the right ways, said *unattainable*. Even her car—an electric blue Aston Martin Vanquish—said *dude, I am so far out of your league, it isn't even funny*.

And so the reasonable thing would have been to just suck it up, get myself an *actual* girlfriend, and pretend that I had never, for even a moment, dreamt of a universe where she and I might have been a thing. But the sad truth was that I had never been able to do it. To walk away from that tiny sliver of possibility. Which meant this was probably going to end in a social disaster of epic proportions. Because hope was such a fragile, dangerous thing to hold on to. *Especially* when you were in a private school filled with the children of diplomats, movie stars, and CEOs.

"*Hellooo*, Earth to Patrick," Connor called out as he waved a hand in front of my face. And that's when I realized I was staring. At her. *Again*.

As I snapped back to reality, I completely missed my locker and instead, slammed my hand into the one next to mine. Nearly managing to drop my book bag on my foot.

"You *really* need to stop staring at the Galathea girl, it's bad for your health," Connor stated with an amused smirk.

"Yeah, I *know*," I agreed regretfully as I shook out my stinging hand. I didn't want to admit that my infatuation with Nualla was getting out of control. But I also couldn't pretend I hadn't gotten a big ass bruise from walking smack into a garbage can the Thursday before winter holiday break either.

Connor tapped out an impatient rhythm on his tablet case before he finally let out a heavy sigh. "We need to get to class; you coming?"

"You go ahead, I'll catch up," I replied, as I tossed my messenger bag into my locker. The first week of the school year our Chem II teacher, Mr. Lucas, had demanded we not bring our bags to Chemistry. Apparently so no one would accidentally trip over them. He had said something to the effect of, "This is chemistry, not physics. We don't need to see what happens when someone falls on their face."

"Well, hurry up. I heard a rumor that Mr. Lucas is switching up our seats again," Connor said before he strode off toward our Chem II class. Mr. Lucas liked to periodically switch our seats and lab partners around so no one got too comfy—or lazy. Today was apparently one of *those* days.

"'Kay," I called back, but he probably hadn't heard me, considering that in a few seconds flat he was already halfway down the hall. But then again, he was a 6'4" black kid, and most of that was legs.

I went back to watching Nualla, whose every movement was like a graceful dance. For nearly four years she had acted like I was invisible. And if it wasn't for the company of my friends, I might even have thought I was a ghost. But not today. Today she had turned when I had called out to her. She had turned...but that was it, and a moment later she was gone again, walking away from me down the hall.

I closed my locker with a heavy sigh. I really couldn't stand around staring anymore, and I would see her in Mr. Lucas' class anyways. So, tablet in hand, I started walking toward class. My eyes fixed on Nualla under the pretense that I was looking at the hallway beyond her. But after only a few steps someone bumped into me as they hurried past. A sudden piercing headache flashed across my eyes, bringing with it a series of blurry, fragmented images, and a strange panic that squeezed my chest like a vice.

I stumbled and dropped my tablet on the white rubber tip of my black All Stars, causing it to skid across the floor. As I bent down to pick it up, I rubbed my temple. Things like this actually happened to me more than I wanted to admit. Though, not enough that I had ever bothered to mention it to my parents. Not that I saw them enough to really mention it in the *first* place.

I stood back up slowly, the world swaying out of kilter, and tried to blink things back into focus. But it seemed to be a lost cause, because everything stayed firmly in the realm of dreamlike blurriness. The hall, and lockers, and remaining students around me seeming much farther away than they should have been.

I blinked a few more times until the world righted itself again into a nauseating clarity, and that's when I finally saw him a short distance in front of me in the nearly vacant hall. Marching purposefully toward Nualla like an angry storm cloud. Michael Tammore. Which probably meant that *he* was the one who had bumped into me.

Figures.

But I really shouldn't have been surprised. Because to say Michael Tammore was a dick would have been a huge understatement. I had absolutely no idea what his parents did for a living, but whatever it was, he somehow felt it gave him the right to treat others like crap. For the most part I avoided him, because one of these days he was going to do something I wouldn't be able to walk away from, and I really, *really* didn't want to get expelled. Because Bayside pretty much had a zero tolerance policy when it came to violence, and I didn't think they'd let me slide if I told them decking Michael was a public service.

And I would have just gone to class and taken some Advil for my increasingly painful headache if it hadn't been for what I saw next.

Apparently today was going to be *that* day.

"I am *so* going to get expelled for this," I said to myself as I marched forward.

The Perils of a High School White Knight

Monday, January 9th

NUALLA

JUST ONE MORE SEMESTER. ONE more semester of pretending I was normal, and then I would be free. One more semester of wearing this mask, and then I could let it go. One more semester of pretending I was like *them*—that I was human.

I had spent the last few years with the secret held close to my heart. A secret that allowed us to pass unnoticed through the human world. The secret of what we *truly* were.

Daemons.

Once, we had been real to them. But in the past millennia, they had carved us so deep into their myths—their fears—that they had distorted us into something that no longer seemed possible.

And so we continued to hide amongst them, flowing through the cracks in their world like water. Filling in the spaces their eyes passed over as they searched for the familiar, the comforting...the safe.

And on the surface we might have looked like them, if no one looked too hard. But one day this perfect mask of lies and natural ability was going to crack, and the truth was going to come spilling out in a way no one would be able to ever hide away again. Because you could only hold your breath for so long before you drowned.

I sucked in a deep breath, letting it out slowly, and gave myself the same pep talk I gave myself every morning.

You can do this. You're a Galathea, and you're not going to be the one who lets them all down, I whispered to myself within my head. And some days this one small thing was all that kept me from screaming the truth to anyone who would listen. Because when the first Grand Council had decided to hide our existence, back when myths were the stuff of truth instead of fairy tales, I doubted they had ever considered the perils of high school. Where just one misplaced step would blow this whole damn charade to shiny bits.

I placed my book bag into my locker slowly, willing my hand to stop shaking. And then I sensed it, a strange yet familiar electricity to the air. I knew what was coming. I always knew with Michael. As good as he was with his illusionary abilities, I could always feel the impact to the air as he prepared to release it.

Oh for frak's sake. Gods, no, not today.

Michael grabbed my arm. "You're going with me to the Winter Ball."

"No, I assure you, I'm *not*," I replied firmly as I jerked away from him. Folding my arms, and glaring at him with contempt.

"Then who are you going with?"

Well *frak.* I hadn't *actually* asked anyone yet.

I looked out past Michael at the nearly vacant hall. The students that were still there were shuffling to their lockers or dashing off to class completely unaware of us. Then again, Michael was using his influence to make them *not* notice us.

"I don't have to tell you," I said, moving my hands to my hips to appear more solid. Even in these boots, Michael was a good five inches taller than me, so I needed all the help I could get.

"I can make you," he said, lifting my chin with his finger so I was forced to look into his eyes.

I pushed him away with all my strength, and tried to step past him. "You wouldn't *dare*."

Michael's illusionary abilities weren't nearly

as potent as his persuasion abilities. And trust me, I had learned *that* one the hard way.

In one swift motion, Michael reached out, and slammed me against the locker. "Enough of your games, Nualla! We both know you are not going to choose a human mate, so why do you keep picking them and not—"

"And not *you*, you mean?" I asked with a derisive snort. "Because I would rather have *anyone's* company than yours. Or hadn't you figured that out yet?"

Michael stood there silently, looking just the slightest bit stunned, but he didn't remove his hold on my shoulders. And the truth was, I could say all the snide things I wanted, but I couldn't get away. He was much stronger than me. He knew it. *I* knew it.

As we stood there like that, the bell rang, and the last remaining students fled the halls. I closed my eyes and made a desperate, silent plea for help even though I knew it was hopeless.

And then something weird happened.

I heard the faintest clatter—nearly inaudible to the human ear—and then an unfamiliar voice demanded, "Get your hands off of her—*now*."

My eyes shot open, and both Michael and I turned in the same moment to stare. In the hall stood a guy I had never seen before. He was solidly built, but definitely not a bodybuilder by any stretch of the imagination. And even though he looked younger than he probably was, there was something in the set of his jaw, and the confidence of his stance, that radiated danger.

"Who the hell are *you*?" Michael asked, in a voice that nearly betrayed just how surprised he was. Which was exactly what *I* was thinking. I had attended Bayside Academy all four years, and didn't remember ever seeing this guy before. And that was saying a lot, considering the school was pretty damn small.

"It doesn't matter who I am, that's no way to treat a girl. *Especially* one who's not your girlfriend," the guy replied, glaring at Michael. The black tangle of hair framing his face making his black-brown eyes seem more dangerous. And I could feel Michael's hold on my shoulders tighten as he looked the guy over.

This guy had found Michael's one fatal flaw—his pride. It was common knowledge that Michael got whatever he wanted. However, only a few people knew that Michael coveted one thing more than anything else on earth. The one thing he couldn't seem to possess. Me. But somehow this guy had figured that out, and had thrown it in Michael's face. The guy was either supremely lucky, or had a death wish.

"I said: Let. Her. *Go*," the mysterious guy demanded, taking a step closer.

"What are you, a white knight or something?" Michael asked with disdain as his hands slipped from my shoulders.

The guy crossed his arms. "When worthless punks like you make me. So yeah, I guess today, I am."

Michael glared at him with a look more deadly than I had ever seen him use. His hands balling up into fists at his sides. And I just gaped at the stranger. He might as well have just poked an enraged tiger with a sharp stick. This was about to get ugly.

"*Excuse me?*" Michael said in a low, deadly voice, shaking with barely contained anger. I was sure Michael had probably never been insulted like that in his entire life, and the shock had already begun to wear off.

"You heard me," the stranger said, standing up a little taller.

He was about an inch or two shorter than Michael, but was built far more solidly—though I doubted this would help him much if they started throwing punches. And so I squeezed my eyes shut, and waited for the sound of fist meeting face.

Oh Fate, Don't Fail Me Now

Monday, January 9th

PATRICK

ICHAEL STARTED TO SWING HIS fist toward me then stopped just as suddenly, looking at something over my shoulder.

It has to be a dirty trick. He's watching for me to look away and then he's going to strike.

But when he just continued to stare, I finally turned. And that's when I saw who was coming down the hall. Mr. Savenrue, my first period Trig teacher.

Well fuck. I really am *going to get expelled today*, I groaned inwardly.

When he was only a few feet from us Mr. Savenrue finally looked up from the tablet in his hands.

"Mr. Tammore, Miss Galathea, what are you doing in the hall? Class started nearly five minutes ago," Mr. Savenrue asked as he looked between the two of them. Then he looked over at me, a look of confusion briefly crossing his face. "Are you new here? I can't seem to remember your name."

"Patrick, Patrick Connolly. I'm in your first period class, sir," I answered, equally confused. I had never missed a single day of his class. I mean sure, Trig was my least favorite class, but I liked Mr. Savenrue, it was halfway through the semester and he hadn't called on me once. It wasn't his fault really that Trig was just about the least interesting thing in the world.

Mr. Savenrue looked at me for a long moment before he stammered uneasily, "Yes—yes, of course you are." And with one more uncertain look at me he broadened his focus to the other two. "Like I asked before, what are the *three* of you doing in the hall?"

"I was *asking* Mr. Tammore to stop harassing Miss Galathea," I answered as as I scowled at Michael.

Mr. Savenrue fixed Michael with a fiery gaze that could have melted ice before he turned his attention to Nualla. "Is this true, Miss Galathea?"

Without missing a beat she answered, "Yes, Mr. Savenrue. Michael was trying to coerce me into going to the Winter Ball with him. I tried to explain I was already going with someone else, but he just wouldn't listen."

"No one asked you yet; you're lying!" Michael growled as he narrowed his eyes at her.

And that's when I kinda lost it. Because the only way I was going to allow him to continue bullying her was over my dead body.

"*I* asked her," I blurted out as I glared at Michael. "*And* she said yes."

Mr. Savenrue put his head in his hand and said with an exasperated huff, "Mr. Tammore, if a girl doesn't want to go with you to a dance, that's her right. You can't always get what you want, you know."

"I usually do," Michael mumbled under his breath.

"What was that, Mr. Tammore?" Mr. Savenrue asked, raising an eyebrow at Michael.

"Nothing, Mr. Savenrue," Michael answered, looking sideways at nothing in particular.

Mr. Savenrue didn't look the slightest bit convinced. "*Hmm*. Well, Mr. Tammore, why don't you accompany me to the dean's office."

At that Michael swallowed hard, and I saw fear flash in front of his eyes for probably the first time ever.

As Mr. Savenrue turned back toward me, I

dropped the smirk from my face as quickly as humanly possible. He reached into his bag, and pulled out two late passes, holding them out to me and Nualla with a strained smile. "Mr. Connolly, Miss Galathea, why don't you head to class."

I just stood there holding that late pass as I watched Michael and Mr. Savenrue walk away, because really, it was one of those what-the-fuck-just-happened? moments.

"So...I'm going with you to the Winter Ball?" Nualla asked as they reached the stairs.

I froze as my heart sputtered to a painful halt. *Oh, fuck me! Did I really just do that? Like for reals?*

I turned slowly as I swallowed hard. And sure enough, she was looking at me expectantly with those beautiful eyes of hers. Periwinkle blue with flecks of silver in them like captured moonlight.

"*Yeah*...about that..." I said as I ran my hand back through my hair nervously. "You were just bluffing, right? 'Cause if you already asked some-one else, you don't have to go with me. I just said that to piss off Michael," I babbled like a total idiot.

Just shut up already. You're only making this worse, you spaz!

"No, you're right, I *was* bluffing. I hadn't actu-ally asked anyone yet," Nualla admitted as she looked away from me, and smoothed the sides of her uniform. Like all the girls at Bayside Academy she wore the standard black V-neck knit sweater over a collared white button-down shirt and black pleated skirt, but on her it looked anything but standard.

God she's so beautiful.

"But I'll go with you—if you ask me that is," Nualla continued as she finally looked back up into my eyes. And she just continued to stare at me, her mouth parted ever so slightly in a way that suddenly filled me with the overwhelming urge to lean down and kiss her.

However, for the first time today, I managed to actually do the *smart* thing, and looked away from her.

Don't fuck this up. You will hate yourself forever if you fuck this up now.

"Nualla, would you go with me to the Winter Ball?" I managed to squeeze past the panicked tightening of my throat as I finally looked back up into her eyes.

Nualla paused for a heartbeat that felt more like a lifetime. "I would love to."

And I just stared at her in disbelief, my mouth hanging open. I had basically been running on an adrenalin-fueled autopilot since I saw the two of them arguing in the hall. However, as she stared up at me expectantly, I was now forced to process the fact that I had just asked Nualla Galathea— *the* Nualla Galathea—to the Winter Ball. Which meant there was no way in *hell* she had actually just said yes...*right*?

As the panicked beating of my heart threatened to knock me senseless I blurted out, "You're serious?"

"Were you serious about asking me?" she asked uncertainly.

"Well yes, of course, but—"

"Then yes, I'm serious, I'll go with you to the dance," she answered as if it was no big deal. Like I was just asking to borrow a pencil or something.

"Um...okay," I said unsteadily as I ran my hand back through my hair again.

"We should probably get to class," Nualla suggested as she started to turn, an amused smile starting to spread its way across her lips.

"Oh yeah, you're probably right," I agreed quickly as I followed along behind her.

Fuck, what am I supposed to do now?

I followed Nualla down the hall toward the Chem classroom, waiting to suddenly wake up and find out this was all just a dream. Or to be struck by lightning, because the universe had realized it had made a horrible mistake. Or *both*.

As we stepped through the classroom door, Mr. Lucas turned to us with an exasperated expression, sucking in breath for a burst of lecture. But before he could get even a single word out we held up our passes.

He let the air out with a sigh and turned back

to what he had been doing. "Thank you for gracing us with your presence. Since you both missed out on today's *earlier* activity, you are now lab partners," he informed us with a huff before he resumed his lecture about today's class work.

As I passed Connor, he arched his eyebrows as if to say, *dude, what the fuck?* And I could only shrug, because really, that's exactly what *I* was trying to figure out.

NUALLA

I T WAS AROUND THE END of Mr. Lucas' lecture when I realized that because of Michael's stupid stunt I had left my tablet in my locker. And because I had already been so hugely late to class there was no way in *hell* he was ever going to let me go get it now.

I put my head in my hands and rubbed my temples. This day was already starting to suck, and it wasn't even close to being lunch yet.

Sometimes universe, you really know how to kick a girl when she's down.

I heard a light clattering, and when I opened my eyes again, a tablet was sitting on the table in front of me.

"You can borrow mine if you like," someone

offered from the seat next to me. I looked up into Patrick's eyes and was lost in the dark beauty of them as he continued, "You forgot to grab yours because of Michael."

"Yeah, I did, didn't I," I agreed breathlessly.

His eyes were deep, almond-shaped pools of nearly black-brown, hinting at a possible heritage. And there was a strange, unique quality to him that made him seem gentle and immediately trustworthy. Which I had to admit made my heart beat uncomfortably fast in my chest. But it was his broad, square-jawed face framed by a tangle of black hair that flared out with a slight curl at his ears that made it beat faster still.

When I just continued to stare at him for way too long, a deep blush spread across his cheeks and he quickly looked toward the smart board at the front of the classroom. And for a while I tried to pay attention to the day's assignment too. But about halfway through the period I finally couldn't restrain myself any longer, and my eyes drifted back to Patrick.

There was something about him…something I couldn't quite put my finger on. But the more I looked at him, the more I wondered why I hadn't noticed him before. How could I have possibly missed a gorgeous boy like this wandering the halls for four straight years? Even if he was terribly shy, I wasn't *that* blind, was I? Maybe he was a new transfer or something.

Better to find out now, one way or the other.

I rested my jaw in my hand and released a bit of my own influence. "So...how long have you been a student at Bayside Academy?" I asked him in my most inviting voice.

Patrick looked up at me in startled confusion. "Four years—why?"

ALTERNATE REALITY

Monday, January 9th

NUALLA

S O WHO ARE YOU GOING to ask to the Winter Ball?" my cousin Nikki asked, staring out at the students around the atrium.

"I already have a date," I replied as I flicked through iTribe on my tablet. I was trying to see if Patrick was in any of the pictures I had taken in the last four years. Maybe he was like a vampire and wouldn't show up in photos. That would explain a lot, really.

"Really? Who?" Nikki asked as she played with the edges of her Norwegian blonde hair.

Her hair had been nearly as long as mine, but she had gotten the bright idea during winter holiday break to cut it in a sharp A-line bob. Now, the back of her hair barely cleared her jaw and the front brushed her chest. And by the way she couldn't stop fiddling with it, I could tell she was rethinking the cut. Probably in about the same way she was rethinking wearing those pale blue thigh-high socks with penguins dancing across them when it was forty-five degrees out. However, I had to admit that the new cut *did* make the natural pale blue streaks in her hair look less...well, out of place. Not every daemon had colored streaks in their hair like us, but it did happen more often in the descendants of the First Families. Which made me wonder what the hell we had all done back before technicolored hair dye became a thing.

"Patrick Connolly," I answered, still flipping through pictures.

"*Who*?" Nikki asked as she dropped her hair and looked at me.

I pointed across the crowded atrium to Patrick. "Him."

"Never seen him before, he a new student or something?" Nikki asked as she looked curiously at Patrick.

I gave up flipping through the photos and rested my chin on my hand. "No, apparently he's been here all four years—which is odd because I can't remember ever seeing him before today. Hell, even Mr. Savenrue didn't remember him, and Patrick's *in* one of his classes."

Nikki stared at me in disbelief. "What?"

"Yeah it's weird, he's in a lot of my classes, but I can't remember seeing him before today."

"That *is* kinda weird," Nikki agreed uneasily as she picked up her soda. She was about to take a sip when she paused. "Hey wait, when did this happen?"

"In the hall right before Chem. Michael was trying to make me go to the dance with him and Patrick stepped in."

"So he saved you from Michael?"

"Yep."

"*Damn* he's good," Nikki said, with a choking laugh. "You should keep him around; Michael repellent is always a good thing to have."

"Ya think?" I said sarcastically.

"Though it was *your* damn fault for dating Michael in the first—"

"Hey, you said you wouldn't pick on me for that anymore!" I said, pushing her.

"Sorry, it's just so hilarious how badly you frakked up there," Nikki laughed, an amused smirk to her lips.

"I *know* I did, so please stop reminding me," I sighed in exasperation. It was nice to see that my screw-ups made for an endlessly entertaining spectacle for my family.

I poked at my lunch as I looked out at Patrick. There was still something about him that seemed so damn… "What nationality do you think he is?"

"A mix," Nikki replied without much thought.

"Well *yeah*, I figured that much. But a mix of what?" I asked as I turned my eyes away from Patrick to Nikki.

"My bet's on some European and Asian," Nikki answered after staring at him a few seconds longer.

Like Travis. Hmmm… "Yeah, I think you're right, Nikki," I agreed before I popped a forkful of chicken Caesar salad into my mouth.

"He's *really* hot," Nikki pointed out, soda half-way to her mouth.

"Hot does not even *begin* to cover that boy," I stated without thinking as I let my eyes trace over his face.

"I *bet* you'd like to cover him," Nikki countered with a mischievous tone to her voice.

And I froze, my fork halfway to my mouth, and looked over at her. She grinned back at me with a devious smile.

"Oh, you wouldn't dare."

Nikki didn't answer, she just grinned even larger.

"Don't you *dare* tell Shawn about—!"

"Tell me what?" Shawn asked as he leaned between us with his tray of food.

"About Nualla's date to Winter Ball," Nikki answered quickly as I made a threatening gesture at her behind his back.

"Really? Who is it this time?" Shawn asked, dropping down onto the bench next to Nikki.

"Patrick Connolly," I answered sourly, jabbing a fork at my lunch. Nikki telling Shawn I had the hots for some guy was slightly above her telling my sister. But not by much.

Shawn paused, his burrito less than an inch from his mouth "Who?"

"*Him*," Nikki said, pointing at Patrick.

Shawn looked over at Patrick, burrito still a few inches from his mouth. "Never seen him before; he new?"

"See what I *mean*? It's like he just appeared out of nowhere," I said in exasperation, throwing my fork down on my plate. This was starting to get really weird, and that was saying a lot coming from people like us.

"Maybe he's here from a parallel universe and just doesn't know it yet," Nikki said, looking at Patrick curiously.

"Nikki, I think you've been watching too much of the SyFy channel," Shawn said, gesturing at her with his lunch.

"Hey, *you* watch it too!" she snapped back indignantly.

PATRICK

THAT GALATHEA GIRL IS CHECKING you out," Connor said, in complete disbelief as he looked past me.

"Really?" I looked up, and sure enough Nualla Galathea, her cousin Nikkalla "Nikki" Varris, and their friend Shawn Vallen were looking at us—at *me* more specifically. The pale January light making them look even paler. Like a handful of students at Bayside Academy, they seemed unusually pale, even for foggy SF. Pale, not in that chalky vampire sort of way, but more in that I'm-Irish-and-have-always-lived-in-Seattle kind of way.

I scooted around the circular lunch table nonchalantly to be able to better look at Nualla without actually appearing to be going out of my way to look at her. As I did, Beatrice scooted to fill my spot without her eyes ever leaving the book in her hands.

"Wonder who she's going with to the dance this time?" Connor said, between bites of his lunch. This speculation had been torture in past years; but not anymore, because I knew who she was going with this time.

"Me."

"In your *dreams*, dude," Connor said, rolling his eyes.

I pulled my eyes away from Nualla to look at him. "No seriously, I'm taking her to the dance."

Connor pointed at me with a french fry. "You're full of it."

"I am not!" I countered indignantly.

"He's telling the truth, I heard Tara Spellman talking about it in third period," Beatrice said, without looking up as she pushed her black cat-eyed glasses back up her short nose.

"How did *she* know about it? I just asked Nualla second period!" I asked, incredulously.

"She overheard you guys on the way to the restroom," Beatrice stated as she took a sip of bottled tea, almond eyes still firmly fixed on her book. She was always reading a book—*always*. I had never seen Beatrice outside of class without one in all the years I had known her.

"What I want to know is how the hell you convinced Nualla Galathea to go with *you*?" Connor asked as he poked me in the shoulder.

"I asked her and she said yes," I answered with a shrug, hoping he'd just drop it. But that was about as likely as an invasion by purple bunnies.

"Seriously? You're telling me you just walked up and asked her after four fucking years of staring at her like a love sick idiot," Connor said as he gave me an unbelievably dubious look.

"No did not just walk up and ask her, I—" I countered indignantly until I realized he had been baiting me into dumping the whole story.

"*Fine.* Look, that prick Michael was trying to bully her into going with him to the dance. So I stepped in and told Mr. Savenrue I was taking her."

"Wait, why was Mr. Savenrue there?" Connor asked in confusion.

"He came down the hall and saw me and Michael arguing. He scolded Michael and took him off to the Dean's office, and sent me and Nualla to class."

"Oh man, *seriously*? I would have paid to see that!" Connor said, laughing.

"Paid to see what?" Jenny, one of our other usual table mates, asked as she walked up with Sara. They placed their lunch trays on the table and sat down.

"Mr. Savenrue berate Michael, and haul him off to the office," Connor answered, barely containing his laughter.

"What did Michael do?" Sara asked, before biting into an apple.

"He was demanding Nualla Galathea go with him to the Winter Ball, but she's already going with Patrick," Beatrice answered, over the top of her book.

"*Really*?" Sara said, nearly choking on a bite of apple, her pale green eyes wide with disbelief.

"Well actually I asked her *after* I told him she was already going with me," I admitted, running my hand back through my hair. The panic that I had *actually* done that still fresh in my mind.

"Well played man, well played," Connor said, clapping me on the shoulder. "That was a gamble you could have lost spectacularly."

"Yeah, tell me something I don't know," I said, with a self-deprecating smile.

"Oh, but I was—" Jenny sputtered, a forkful of Caesar salad halfway to her mouth. Then her ice blue eyes narrowed. "Wait, I thought you had never talked to her before?"

"Well no, not before today at least," I admitted reluctantly.

Geez, if even my friends didn't believe me, how was anyone *else* ever going to?

"And she said yes?" Jenny asked, in complete disbelief.

"Of *course* she did. She had the choice between Michael and Patrick. Who the hell do you *think* she would pick?" Connor said, gesturing to me.

"Thanks Connor, that's not really a winning endorsement you know," I said, flatly.

Sometimes I thought I must just be a big joke to my friends. I really couldn't blame them though. I mean I *had* been pining for a girl who was way out of my league for the last four years. But now that I had a shot with her—albeit a slight shot—I was at a loss as to what I should do next. I had to play my cards just right, or I was going to go down in flames.

"So you were late to chem class because you

were asking her?" Sara asked, looking at me inquiringly.

"Yeah, among other things," I answered, coughing.

"That's right, she's your Chem partner now too, huh?" Connor said as he nudged me.

"Yep," I answered with a huge grin.

"Bet you're *really* glad now you didn't take Field Biology," Beatrice said, smirking over her book.

"Hey, there's nothing wrong with Biology!" Jenny said, indignantly.

"Yeah, but in Chem you get to blow things up," Connor pointed out as he demonstrated an explosion with his hands.

Jenny glared at Connor a moment longer before she huffed and shoved a forkful of salad in her mouth.

Connor grinned in triumph before he turned his attention back to me. "So, Patrick, is Nualla Galathea everything you'd thought she'd be?"

Here Goes Nothing

Monday, January 9th

PATRICK

WHEN I GOT HOME, I finally gave myself permission to freak out. In fact, I spent a good hour staring at my ceiling in shock. Flung out on my bed like I was trying to make a snow angel.

I had actually gotten up the courage to ask Nualla Galathea out, and even more shocking she had actually said *yes*. But the problem was, I had spent so long wishing that this would happen, I hadn't given much thought to what I would do if it actually *did*. Which meant if there was a higher power out there, they were probably laughing their ass off at me right now.

The whole thing was so fucking surreal that I was beginning to wonder if I had hallucinated the whole thing. What if some part of my brain had just snapped? I mean, I *had* been feeling really ill as I walked toward them in the hall. What if I was actually in a hospital somewhere right now in a coma?

Okay, you're being crazy. Just calm the fuck down and take a breath.

But even if it *was* all real, there were so many ways this could go wrong it wasn't even funny. It wasn't as if I had dated a whole lot of girls and would know what I was supposed to do. Knowing my luck, I was probably going to manage to fuck things up in the first five minutes of our date.

I tried to calm myself again. *Just play it cool, Patrick. It's not like you're dating her or anything. You're just going to one dance.*

But what if we *were* dating now? What if she was sitting at home right now waiting for me to change my iTribe status? Or worse, what if this was all just a big prank and my classmates were on there right now making fun of my stupidity?

The sick fear of uncertainty and self-doubt began to twist my stomach into knots. For better or worse, I had to know one way or the other.

With a shaking hand, I reached over and picked up my phone.

Here goes nothing.

I looked down at my page, swallowing hard.

And was a little surprised to find there was already a friend request from Nualla waiting for me.

> HEY STRANGER, THOUGHT I'D BETTER ADD YOU AS A FRIEND ON HERE. HOPE YOU DON'T MIND.
> —NUALLA

I don't think I had ever clicked a confirm button so fast in my life. But then I just sat there staring at the screen, trying to figure out just what exactly I was supposed to do next.

Hours later I finally decided to just roll with the punches. I mean, what was the worst that could happen...right?

NUALLA

WHAT YA DOING?" NIKKI ASKED as she flopped down on my bed and used my back as a pillow.

"Looking up mystery boy online," I answered as I continued flipping through pictures of Patrick at some event at a mall. A few hours of online investigation had turned up quite a lot about Patrick Connolly; the boy practically lived his life online. Forum posts, videos, pictures, and social media up the wazoo. He seemed to take pictures of everything around him, and I had to admit I was a little envious of how freely he could share his life with others. I, on the other hand, had to keep most of the things about myself private, hidden, secret. Like a CIA agent or a superhero, but without the awesome costume or badge.

"Find anything good?" Nikki asked as she turned her head to look at me.

"He is *unbelievably* geeky," I answered with a crooked grin as a new picture of him slid onto screen.

"Like more than me and Shawn?"

"*Totally* more than you and Shawn," I answered as I held the tablet out for her to see.

"He does cosplay?" Nikki commented with arched eyebrows. Cosplay was one of those things Nikki had discovered freshman year when we first came to a human school, and to say she was a little obsessed was a huge understatement.

"Apparently."

"Does he have any without a shirt on?" Nikki asked as she flipped through the event pictures.

"*No*," I answered with a sigh.

"You *totally* checked didn't you?" Nikki said with a laugh as she grinned at me.

"Oh, no, you do *not* get to tease me girl-who-has-never-had-a-date," I said as I arched my back and pulled my legs into a kneeling position.

Nikki scowled at me as she let the tablet drop onto the bed. "So what if I haven't. I'm waiting for the right person."

The *right* person for Nikki was Shawn and it always had been. And it was driving me up the wall waiting for them to get their shit together and figure it out.

"Seriously, will you just admit you—" *totally like Shawn.* Nikki just stared at me with wide eyes as she waited for me to continue. "You know what, never mind," I humphed as I let myself fall back into my pillows.

"Not everyone can be like you, Nualla," Nikki said quietly after a few moments of silence. And it was what she *didn't* say, that made me realize I was kinda being a jerk. She was afraid to fall in love, simple as that. And Nikki, more than anyone else I knew, had every reason to be. Because it hadn't *exactly* worked out too well for her mom, my aunt Skye.

I let out a heavy sigh, "Sorry."

"I'm used to it by now," Nikki said with a shrug.

"I'm still sorry."

"Well *sorry* owes me something shiny then," Nikki said as she crawled across the bed, and leaned against the headboard next to me.

"How about I get you your Winter Ball dress?" I offered.

"I'm not *going* to the dance, Nualla," Nikki

replied with a sigh.

"Sure you are," I countered, looking over at her.

"I don't even have a date," Nikki stated as she blew her bangs out of her eyes with huff.

"'Course you do—Shawn."

"I'm not going with Shawn. I mean it's not like he's *asked* me or anything," Nikki said dismissively as she played with the edges of her hair again.

"Nikki, when has Shawn ever *not* gone with you?"

"Well maybe he's going with someone else this time."

"Like *who*? Shawn doesn't even *talk* to other girls."

"He talks to Natalie," Nikki countered as she continued to stare fixedly at the edges of her hair.

"Only because he's known her like, forever."

"Nualla, he's known *us* like, forever," Nikki pointed out as she finally turned to look at me.

"Will you just *ask* him? Cause if you don't, I'm going to ask him *for* you," I threatened as I folded my arms across my chest.

Nikki's mouth dropped open. "You wouldn't."

"Oh, you know I will," I replied, arching one eyebrow.

Nikki scowled at me before she let out an irritated huff. "*Fine*. I'll ask him."

"Better do it quick, because if you don't do it

by lunch tomorrow, *I'll* do it.

"I get it, okay, *geez*," Nikki grumbled as she pulled out her phone and started texting. "Here, distract yourself before you do any *more* damage," Nikki said as she pushed my tablet toward me.

"Don't mind if I do," I said smugly as I continued my online investigation of Patrick Connolly.

"So, you learn anything *else* about Patrick other than he looks good in really tight pants?" Nikki asked sarcastically as she tapped away at her phone screen.

"'Course I did, boy practically lives his life online," I answered with a snort.

"Did he draw that?" Nikki asked as she looked down at the picture I had on screen.

"Yep."

"Whoa, he is like seriously good," Nikki admitted with wide eyes.

I flipped through a few more of Patrick's drawings before Nikki asked, "Does he draw fan art?"

"Maybe *you* two should go out instead," I said teasingly as I leaned in to look at her text.

"He's not my type," Nikki replied as she jerked her phone out of my view.

"And what *is* your type?" I asked teasingly.

Nikki just stared back at me with a deer-in-headlights sort of look before her phone emitted a loud ding.

"Bet that's Shawn confessing his undying love for you."

"Shut up, Nualla," Nikki said as her eyes darted down to her phone. She stared at it for a long moment before she finally spoke. "He said yes," she breathed, sounding more than a little surprised.

"Of *course* he did," I snorted, rolling my eyes.

Secrets and Small Talk

Tuesday, January 10th

PATRICK

O KAY, DON'T FREAK OUT. *IT'S just a girl. A girl you've basically had the serious hots for since the first day of Freshman year.*

Oh, I was so going to fuck this up.

"Hey," a warm female voice greeted me.

I sat up straight quickly—*too* quickly—and slammed my knee into the leg of the chem lab table.

"Hey," I echoed, trying to conceal my grimace of pain.

"You're here early," Nualla commented with a hint of surprise to her voice.

I froze, finally realizing the flaw in my plan.

Oh, fuck.

"Yeah, I needed to finish the homework from yesterday." Which wasn't entirely a lie. I had been a little behind because I had loaned her my tablet all period, but I had just copied Connor's notes.

Nualla looked at me curiously for a moment before something seemed to occur to her. "Oh gods, I'm sorry," Nualla replied as she slipped onto her lab stool. Her knees brushing against my thigh as she turned.

"It's uh...it's okay. I think I was able to get it all done anyways."

"Well, here's my notes from yesterday just in case," Nualla offered as she slid her tablet toward me.

"Thanks," I replied with a strained grin. Now I was going to have to copy them all down so she wouldn't realize I was a complete fucking liar.

I opened a blank page on my tablet and started transcribing her notes.

"You didn't get *any* notes done at all yesterday," she asked in disbelief.

"I...uh...not exactly."

Nualla gave me a sympathetic look. "I'll just send you mine okay?"

"Okay."

"What's your iTribe email?" Nualla asked as she pulled her black and lapis blue hair into a high ponytail, exposing the soft pale flesh of her neck.

And I had to fight a strong, nearly overwhelming desire to run my fingers over her exposed skin.

What the hell is wrong with you? I admonished myself as I dug my fingernails into my palms until they hurt.

Nualla looked over at me as she dropped her hands, and noticed I was watching her.

Say something—anything!

"That's a cool pendant," I blurted out. And it was.

It was a weird sort of silver circular pendant a little bigger than a quarter. It looked Egyptian with a gazelle-horned deity, her hands held outstretched at her sides, a small crescent moon resting between her horns. A deep lapis blue enameled background covered with tiny silver stars filled the space behind her, and a larger crescent encircled the whole design. An inscription ran across the outer crescent, but the symbols didn't look Egyptian; they looked like something else—something I could almost remember.

"Thanks," Nualla answered with a small nervous smile.

"Where'd you get it?"

"My...my dad gave it to me when I was little," she answered, a flicker of unease crossing her face as she quickly tucked it back beneath her uniform.

"My mom gave me a pendant too," I said as my hand went up to my neck. And then I remembered like a total idiot that I had managed to lose it the day before.

"Really?" Nualla asked, looking at my bare neck.

"But I...I apparently lost it yesterday."

"Oh."

"So now it feels way weird because I've been wearing it as long as I can remember. And I still haven't told—" And that's when I realized I was babbling like an idiot. "—my mother."

Nualla opened her mouth to say something, but she never got the chance, because Mr. Lucas walked in and dropped his bag on his desk.

"Good morning, class. Did everyone turn in their assignments yet?" he asked as he scanned the room and was met with complete silence. "No? Well you have five minutes left to do so before I start marking them down," Mr. Lucas informed us before he turned his back on the class and started uploading the day's assignment to the smart board.

"Guess you better turn yours in," Nualla said as she looked over at me.

"Yeah," I agreed breathlessly.

Nualla looked at me expectantly and I just stared back at her.

"I still need your iTribe email address."

"My email?" I asked in confusion.

"So I can send you my notes," Nualla said like I was a bit slow.

"Oh, right, sorry," I said quickly, snapping out of my daze. There was something about her eyes that was wildly distracting this close up. "It's PatrickC8."

"Why eight?" Nualla asked curiously as she emailed me the notes.

"I don't know, I just kinda like the number eight I guess," I said with a nervous shrug.

As we studiously worked through the day's assignment, I couldn't help but stare a Nualla. Even after hours online looking through her iTribe page, I hadn't learned a whole lot about her. Sure, there were photos, but not a whole lot, and nothing that really revealed that much about her that I didn't already know.

So all I had to go on was what I had learned from just observing her in class these past few years. A lot of little things that added up to a very interesting picture—well, at least to me anyways. But the sparseness of her iTribe page made me start to wonder. I couldn't believe that she didn't lead an interesting life, so why didn't she post any of it? It almost seemed like the bits that were online were just for show. Like they were there just so people wouldn't look any farther. Which made me really start to wonder if she had something she was trying to hide from me. Or her parents. Or the world.

I had this nagging feeling I couldn't seem to shake screaming at me in the back of my mind that there was something different about her. Something hiding behind those eyes. A secret that would reveal itself to me if I just studied her harder. If I just put all the tiny little pieces back together in the right order. The secret of who Nualla Galathea *really* was.

Just Smile and Wave

Friday, January 13th

NUALLA

"I STILL DON'T SEE WHY SHAWN couldn't have driven us to the mall," Nikki whined as we walked down Powell Street. The street was a beast with one of the steepest hills in the City, but we were nearly finished walking down the worst part now. It wasn't so bad to drive down, but walking was kinda a bitch. Especially in three inch boots when it was threatening to rain.

"Because then he'd want to come with us," I replied before taking a sip of my coffee, the hot liquid warming my chest on its way down.

"*And*?"

"And we are going dress shopping, Nikki. You

don't want him to see you in the dress before you wear it to the dance. It's bad luck," I said as I stopped at the corner to wait for the light to change.

"I'm fairly certain that is just for weddings, Nualla," Nikki pointed out as the light turned green.

"Whatever, you'll thank me later," I said as I started across the street.

"We could have had an Embassy car pick us up."

"Uck no. I feel like enough of a freak most of the time without a black diplomatic town car picking me up at school, thank you very much."

"What about Travis?" Nikki suggested as we started down the next hill.

"He doesn't get off until six."

"Oh, and like he wouldn't just leave work early to drive you wherever you wanted," Nikki stated skeptically.

I stopped walking, and glared at her. "It's just a few frakkin' blocks Nikki, it's not going to kill you."

"I don't know, it *might*," Nikki grumbled as big, fat drops of rain started to pelt the sidewalk around us.

I looked back over my shoulder at her. "You are not the Wicked Witch of the West so just suck it up and—" I started to say as my boot hit a sleek patch of ground. Instinctually, my lightning-fast reflexes kicked in, and I landed in a comfortable crouch, not a drop of coffee spilled. Which was both a blessing and a curse. I hadn't spilled my coffee all over myself, but no human on earth could move as fast as I just did.

Oh frak!

I looked around without moving my head, my heart beating frantically in my chest. Dozens of people were flat out gawking at me.

Frak! Frak! Frak!

A guy just in front of us, pizza in hand, spoke first. "Jesus girl, are you a gymnast or something?"

Nikki grabbed my arm, pulling me to my feet and flashed a radiant smile at the guy. And I could feel her influence hit him like a Mack truck. "No, she's a martial arts champion."

The guy must have bought the story, because he smiled and continued walking down the street.

"Martial arts champion?" I said, questioningly.

"Your boobs are *way* too big for you to be a gymnast. Martial Arts was the only thing I could think of," she answered with a shrug.

"*Right,*" I said, rolling my eyes. My boobs *were* noticeably a bit too big for my frame, but she really didn't need to point it out every chance she got.

I looked around, everyone else on the busy

street had continued on their way paying us no mind. Well *almost* everyone at least. Patrick— who had apparently been walking down the street behind us—just stared at me, his mouth hanging open just a bit and his eyes wide with surprise. I would have thought he was following us if it wasn't for the fact that the mall was at the end of the street.

"Oh *frak*, he totally saw that," I cursed, turning back around quickly.

"Who?" Nikki asked, looking around.

"Patrick."

Nikki looked over my shoulder completely failing at being nonchalant. "Oh, yeah, *totally*," Nikki agreed with a snort.

"What do I do?" I asked in a panic.

"Wave?" Nikki suggested with a shrug.

PATRICK

THIS WEEK WAS QUITE POSSIBLY the best week of my entire life, hands down. And even though I was walking down what was quite possibly the steepest street in SF, without an umbrella and the skies overhead threatening to dump a deluge on me, I couldn't manage to wipe the smile from my face. Because Nualla Galathea knew I existed. And even though talking to her filled me with a slightly nauseating excitement, I wouldn't trade it for the world. Because Nualla was...

...right in front of me.

I stopped abruptly when I realized the girl with long black hair walking beside a girl in a matching Bayside Academy uniform about a hundred feet in front of me were Nualla and her cousin Nikki.

Why was Nualla walking down the street? She had what was arguably the most awesome car to *ever* park in the student lot at Bayside, so why was she walking?

As I ran through scenarios and reasons in my head Nualla turned around slightly to say something to Nikki. And that's when I realized what was about to happen. I opened my mouth to call out to her even though I knew it was going to be too late.

Nualla slipped, her feet coming off the ground almost comically and I cringed because I knew what was going to happen next. I had seen enough people hit that metal plate enough times on my way to the mall. But this time it didn't happen quite like I expected. Faster than humanly possible, Nualla managed to twist her body in a way that ended with her in a flawless crouch, coffee cup still perfectly in hand.

I dropped my coffee. *That was...impossible.*

I continued to blink at Nualla, unable to believe what I had just seen as Nikki pulled Nualla to her feet. After a short conversation with some guy on the street, Nualla finally looked up in my direction and froze, our eyes locking, before she turned quickly away. A few words passed between the two of them before Nikki looked past Nualla in my direction. And shrugging, she started to wave at me. Nualla stormed off across the street as I waved back at Nikki, a little too stunned to do anything else.

What. The. Actual. Fuck?

As I stood there in the rain waving like an idiot, the realization that there really *was* something different about Nualla hit me like a brick to the head. She was hiding something behind those beautiful eyes of hers, and I intended to figure out exactly what *it* was.

Do I Make You Nervous?

Friday, January 13th

NUALLA

O
H, MY GODS. THIS IS so not happening," I
breathed out as I looked through the hanging jewelry of the kiosk to see Michael
standing about fifty feet away.

"Excuse me?" the kiosk girl asked in confusion.

"Oh, uh, nothing," I blurted out quickly as I
dropped down and and pretended to tie my boot.

Frak! Frak! Frak!

As if nearly blowing my cover in front of
Patrick wasn't bad enough, now I had to deal
with *this* crap? *Seriously, universe, you suck!*

I needed a place to hide—like *fast.* My eyes

darted frantically around until I saw a bookstore a short distance away.

Perfect!

I chanced a quick glance in Michael's direction. Fortunately, he was looking the other way. And so I took a deep breath, and walked as quickly to the bookstore as I could without attracting too much unwanted attention. I really did *not* want to have to deal with Michael, especially outside of school where he was less likely to get in trouble for harassing me. The boy just didn't seem to understand the word "over."

I reached the bookstore, and quickly stepped behind a front display shelf. I would be fine as long as he didn't come in here. I took another deep breath, and peered over the top of the shelf into the mall's common area.

"Is he bothering you again?" someone asked quietly from behind me.

I jerked up with a start, whipping my head around, and was met with kind brown eyes. Brown eyes that were starting to become *very* familiar.

Patrick?

"What, are you following me or something?" I snapped defensively. Between him seeing me exhibiting some not-so-human traits and Michael all but stalking me, I was a little bit on edge.

"No actually, I come here nearly every day," he

countered, looking a bit wary of my harsh tone. "You sure you're not following *me*?"

I opened my mouth to say something, but caught sight of Michael looking in our direction. I grabbed Patrick's hoodie, and crouched down behind the short shelf of books.

Patrick looked at me, raising an eyebrow. "I'll take that as a yes."

"*Yes,* he's bothering me," I answered, peeking around the corner of the bookcase.

After a minute or so of silence Patrick asked, "What's in the bag?"

I turned my head quickly back toward him, meeting his eyes, and almost wished I hadn't. His eyes were the type of brown that was nearly black; deep pools that looked like they would swallow me if I looked too long.

I realized I had been holding my breath, and let it out in an audible puff. "Huh?"

"The bag," Patrick said as he pointed at the dress bag next to me.

I looked down at it then back up at him. "A dress."

"Is it the one you're going to wear to the dance?" he asked as he peered a little closer at the bag.

"Yeah," I answered cautiously.

"Can I see it?"

"*No,* I want it to be a surprise," I answered indignantly before I scooted away from him to get a better look outside the window. Michael was still standing just outside the store, and seemed to be having a heated conversation with someone on the other end of the phone.

Come on Michael, go check out the food court or the theater, anything *that gets me out of here without running into you.*

"What does he want, anyways?" Patrick asked, leaning over me to peer around the bookcase.

"Me," I replied without pulling my eyes from the window.

"Well I can see why," Patrick said matter-of-factly.

That got my attention, and I turned quickly around to face him. "*Excuse me?*"

Patrick's expression looked queasy, pained even—like he hadn't meant for the words to actually be spoken out loud. "Oh wow, that sounded way stalkerish didn't it?"

"Yeah, just a bit. But it's okay. No one really says nice things like that to me."

"Really? I would think guys would be falling all over themselves to tell you you're pretty."

"You might think that, but you'd be wrong," I answered as I chanced a peek around the shelf again. Michael was still talking on the phone, but had moved a few feet farther away.

"I think I make them nervous," I said in a small voice. I had begun to notice it the older I got, how people—even my *own* people—treated me differently.

"Oh, I can definitely understand that," Patrick said with a slight smile in his voice.

I turned back to face him. "Do I make *you* nervous?" He stared at me open-mouthed, like he was unsure of what he should say. "I'll take that as a yes," I said flatly.

"Okay, you do—a little—okay, *a lot*. It's just that—" Patrick stammered, a blush spreading across his cheeks.

"Can I help you two with something?" someone asked from behind us.

I looked up to see a very bored, college-aged guy, staring down at us over a stack of books in his hands. "Um..." I looked out the window again in time to see Michael going down the escalator. "Nope we're good," I answered quickly as I stood up, grabbed Patrick's hand, and walked swiftly toward the exit.

Patrick let me drag him for several feet before he asked, "So by our quick escape I'm guessing Michael's gone somewhere else?"

"You would be correct."

I whipped out my phone, and quickly texted Nikki as I walked. Looking up every few seconds to make sure I didn't run into anyone.

Please have found your phone by now Nikki, I pleaded to myself as I tapped at the screen.

After we had left the dress shop on our way to the food court, Nikki had realized she had left her phone in the dressing room and had dashed back to get it while I stopped at that kiosk.

Today 5:18 pm
Nualla Galathea

Michael's here want to get out of town?

I wove around a pack of stroller moms, but didn't lessen my pace. I just hoped Patrick wouldn't think I was a complete lunatic, but after what he had seen happen between Michael and me this week, I kinda doubted he would. But still, somehow what he thought of me mattered, maybe a little more than it should have.

My phone buzzed and I looked down at it again.

Today 5:23 pm
Nikki Varris

Sure I'll call Shawn & tell him to pick us up out front k.

It was then that I realized I was still dragging Patrick through the mall. I stopped and turned a little too suddenly, his hand still in mine. Unable to stop his momentum, he ran straight into me, and we crashed to the floor.

Sigh. I really needed to stop forgetting just

how much slower human reactions were to ours.

Patrick looked at me in horror—his legs straddling my hips— before he quickly got back to his feet.

I just had to smile at him because he looked so embarrassed even though it was completely my fault.

"Wanna get out of here?" I asked, broadening my smile.

After a short pause his lips slid into a grin, and he offered his hand to me. "Sure, why not."

Once back on my feet, we all but sprinted to the exit.

Let's Get Out
of This Town

Friday, January 13th

PATRICK

WHEN NUALLA HAD ASKED IF I wanted to get out of here, I hadn't considered that she had meant to another state. Which was why it had come as a total shock when I found myself standing near a ticket counter in SFO, staring at Nualla as she watched the flight information flash across the screens.

After our daring escape from the mall, we had blazed a trail out of the city and down 101 to SFO. I was so caught up in the laughter of diving into a car just as Michael came out the mall doors after us, that I didn't even notice we were going to the airport. I actually got all the way into the terminal before I even acknowledged anything other than the fact that I was with Nualla and we weren't at school. Even when I finally looked around and saw where we were, I thought it was a joke, until I remembered I was with a bunch of super-rich kids. And "out of town" to them meant something completely different.

But I was already in too deep by this point, and I *really* didn't want to bail. I just prayed that they would at least keep it in the country, because I didn't *actually* have a passport. As I fidgeted nervously, I silently calculated how much money I had in my bank account. I really didn't want to have to look like a dork for being too broke to buy my ticket to whatever crazy place they were planning to run off to.

"So where are we going, cuz?" Nikki asked Nualla, who was still staring up at the flight board.

"Wherever has a flight leaving first," Nualla answered without looking away from the board.

Nikki raised an eyebrow. "We running from something?"

Parents. Homework. Nualla's stalker punk. Life. Any one of these things seemed like perfectly logical things to run from.

Nualla eyed me covertly as she answered her cousin. "Naw, just looking for a bit of fun."

As she whipped her head back around to look at the board, her hair to flung out just like in a movie.

God she's beautiful.

How the hell had I gotten so lucky to end up here with them—with *her*? Maybe I had been hit by a bus and I was in a coma, dreaming. Or dead.

No, as unbelievable as this all was, I knew it was reality because, A: my fantasies weren't this delusional. And B: I had absolutely no idea what the inside of an airport looked like in real life—well, until now anyways.

While I was contemplating my sanity and luck, Nualla had apparently made her decision because she walked over to the ticket counter to purchase our tickets.

Shawn looked up at the flight board. "My money's on New York."

"Hawaii," Nikki chimed in cheerfully.

"LA," I guessed without even looking.

Nualla returned a few minutes later holding four tickets and thrust them toward us. "Vegas," she said with finality.

NUALLA

"V EGAS? *REALLY?*" NIKKI ASKED ME as we walked through one of the airport terminal shops that offered clothing, because I'd be damned if I was going to wear my Bayside Academy uniform to a dance club.

"Why not?" I shouted back over my shoulder as I pushed past a particularly hideous poncho thing.

"Because aren't we supposed to be meeting Travis at Lunaris tonight?"

"*And?*" I asked, finally stopping and turning to look at her.

"*Nualla*," Nikki sighed in exasperation as she leaned against a display. "You know if you do anything that would wind up in *Secrets*, your dad is going to be pissed."

"When have I ever—?"

Nikki gave me a look, and I shut my mouth. The Minors Privacy Act had probably saved me in the past, but it wasn't going to do squat now that I was eighteen.

I let out a tortured sigh, and leaned against the display next to Nikki. "I promise not to get up on the bar if you promise—"

"Oh, so now *I'm* making promises?" Nikki snorted with arched eyebrows as she folded her arms across her chest.

"—to stop me if I try to get up on the bar."

Nikki looked at me for a long moment before she sighed. "*Fine.* I promise to try to stop you from doing anything that will bring shame to all of Karalia."

"Good then, moving on," I said gleefully with a huge grin as I walked into the ladies clothing section of the shop.

"Did you at *least* text Travis and let him know we aren't coming?" Nikki asked as she followed behind me. "Because he is going to be more than pissed when he shows up and we aren't there."

"*Yes.*"

"*Really*?" Nikki asked dubiously.

"Okay, *fine*, I didn't. But I am right now," I said as I waved my phone at her.

"Nualla, he…" Nikki started in a weird voice, and I looked up. But instead of continuing she just sighed and looked away. "You sure you know what you're doing?"

"Nope, but that just makes it more fun," I answered as I finished texting Travis.

Slipping my phone back into my book bag, I looked at the selection of ladies clothing. The clothing in front of me was less than club worthy, that's for sure.

I ran my teeth over my bottom lip. "Hey, Nikki, do you think they have scissors?"

PATRICK

I DON'T KNOW WHY I had been so cocky in the bookstore. I never thought I would be saying those things to her; not even in my wildest dreams. Maybe that was why I had said it; my brain was convinced I was dreaming. *You really can't fuck up in a dream, so what's to lose, right?* is what was running through my head as I waited for the girls to change from their school uniforms into normal clothes.

I leaned against the wall and let my head fall back, letting out a deep breath.

"Sorry I didn't bring you anything dude, Nikki didn't mention you would be coming," Shawn Vallen said, apologetically.

I looked at him with a half-smile. He was much taller than me—like Connor, somewhere in the 6'1" to 6'4" range. Though unlike Connor, Shawn wasn't wiry like a runner. Instead, Shawn had the broad shoulders and solid build of a warrior with a sharply planed face like a cheetah. And a tangle of wavy blond hair roughly the same shade of blond as Nikki's, which spilled over his forehead nearly to his eyes and curled over the tops of his ears.

"Don't worry about it; I don't think she even knew I was coming."

Shawn cocked his head to one side, and smiled

a crooked smile at me. "You're playing it cool, but you're scared shitless, aren't you?"

"Is it that obvious?" I asked, with a weak, self-deprecating smile.

"Naw, if you weren't scared, I'd know you were a conceited wank."

"*What*?" I said, nearly choking.

"The biggest pricks act all smooth in front of girls because they think they're the shit. You, on the other hand..."

"Ah. But you seem calm, what's that say about you?" I countered.

"Me? Well, I've known those two my whole life. They know about all the stupid shit I've ever done. Hard to be nervous anymore at that point," Shawn answered, looking into the distance.

"Yeah, you're probably right."

"Look, don't worry about it so much. Just relax," he advised, looking back at me with a smile.

"Easy for you to say," I said, running my hand back through my hair.

"Just think about it like hanging out with friends after school, nothing serious."

"I really don't hang out with my friends that much after school. Honestly, most of the time I'm alone," I admitted without thinking.

"Dude, *seriously*? That's really sad."

"Yeah I know," I agreed, leaning my head back against the wall again. I don't know why I was being so honest about how truly lame I was; it wasn't going to help me.

"But I really can't say I'm much better. I mostly hang out with those two girls. Can't remember ever having many guy friends," Shawn admitted, folding his arms across his chest.

"I'd be your friend," I blurted out without giving it much thought.

Wow, did I really just say that out loud? God, he probably thinks I'm even lamer now than he did before.

"Really? Coolness, friendship accepted," Shawn said, with a huge grin.

Wait, what?

But I really didn't have time to think about it long, because something hit me in the chest. I looked down at the floor at some clothes that had apparently been thrown at me.

"Nualla, you're supposed to say 'think fast' *before* you do that, not just throw things at people," Shawn said as he pushed away from the wall.

"What are these?" I asked, bending down to pick up the clothing.

"They're clothes, silly. You didn't think we would really make you go to Vegas in your Bayside Academy uniform, did you?"

Actually, that's completely what I had thought, but thanks for having a higher opinion of me than I do.

I looked at the clothes again; they were super stylish designer casual, and probably cost a small fortune since we were at an airport. "Thanks. How much were they, I'll pay you back," I said, looking up.

"Don't worry about it," Nualla said with a broad smile. "Think of it as payment for letting me kidnap you this weekend."

Aside from her black pleated skirt that seemed to be far shorter than I remembered, her Bayside uniform had been replaced with a electric blue tank top and a black I <3 SF T-shirt that had had a pair of scissors taken to it. What had probably once been a normal T-shirt was now hanging off her shoulders and slashed down both sides so the brilliant blue tank showed through.

"Okay, then how much were the tickets?" I asked, unable to stop looking at just how much of her legs was showing now that her black leggings had gone the way of her school uniform.

"Don't kidnappers usually pay for the transportation of the kidnapped?" Nualla asked as she leaned in closer—*dangerously* closer.

"Um...yeah, but really, I can't just—"

"Dude, you're never going to win this, so just give up," Shawn said, nudging me.

"Okay," I said uneasily.

"Now go change, our plane's gonna start boarding soon," Nualla said with a smile as she pushed me toward the restrooms.

I took a few steps then stopped.
Wait, weekend?

RAISE YOUR GLASS

Friday, January 13th

PATRICK

VEGAS WAS...SHINY. THAT WAS really the only word for it. I honestly didn't think I had ever seen so many lights in my life. It seemed like they basically lit up every inch of the city they possibly could. Their power bills must have been astronomical. It felt like we had entered a theme park for adults. I had seen this place a lot of times on TV, but it just didn't do it justice. And all I could do was stare out the window as we passed a pyramid, a castle, and even the Statue of Liberty.

I didn't ask where we were going, and honestly, I didn't even notice where we were until a bouncer asked for IDs.

Crap! I didn't *have* a fake ID.

I turned to Nualla to mention this, but without missing a beat she handed the bouncer four IDs and smiled. He looked at them for a second seeming a little dazed. And I thought we were screwed at that point—that any second he was going to call the cops. I mean that's what they did when minors tried to get into nightclubs, right? But to my utter disbelief, he handed the IDs back to her, and stepped aside to let us pass.

Just inside the door a smiling hostess took our bags and handed all of us little keychain key cards.

"What's this?" I asked, looking at it questioningly.

"It's your Eclipse card; it tracks your drink purchases, so you don't have to carry around your belongings while you're here," the hostess answered, with a cheery smile.

"*Really*?" I said, examining the card more closely. "That's awesome."

"Just tap it here and press your thumb in the sensor," the hostess instructed as she gestured to a machine beside her. "Oh, and please don't lose it, or we will be forced to charge you the maximum limit."

"Oh really, what's that?" I asked as I pressed my thumb against the reader.

"You *really* don't want to know," Nualla

answered quickly, pushing me gently away from the door.

"Enjoy your night, Miss Galathea," the hostess called behind us.

"Wait, Why does she know your—?"

"Just keep walking," Nualla replied as she tried to move me into the club faster.

I looked back at her uneasily and wondered just how many times you had to come to a place like this before they remembered your name.

Being that I was in high school and had obviously never *been* to a club before, I only had movies and episodes of *CSI* to go from. So I was pretty sure most clubs didn't actually look like the ones on TV. However, this one *totally* did.

The place was filled with light-up dance floors, multiple levels, swirling flashing lights, and music you could feel through your body. Oh, and swarms of people pressed together. Their bodies pulsing with the music. The lights washing everyone in a golden-red light like—well like an eclipse actually. And as we wove through the crowds of people to an empty table I tried not to gape at it all like an idiot. But I'm pretty sure I looked like a fish with its mouth hanging open.

A drink girl passed us, and Nualla said

something to her that I couldn't hear above the music. The girl nodded at whatever Nualla had said, and walked off.

"Pretty awesome place," I said loudly as I looked around.

"You've never been to a club before, have you?" Shawn asked, with a smirk.

"Nope."

"Awesome! Then this should be even *more* fun," he said, smiling mischievously. Something in his expression told me he was sharing a private joke with himself.

The drink girl placed some shots in front of us, and Nualla tapped her card on the drink tray sensor. It flashed green, and the girl walked away, disappearing into the throng of people.

"Bottoms up," Shawn said as he raised his shot glass.

I just stared at mine. People—mostly parents—liked to pretend that high school kids didn't drink. They were completely wrong of course, but they could keep deluding themselves if they liked.

I was by no means a lush or a teenage alcoholic, but I also was not a stranger to the stuff, either. I had thought that my parents might have noticed at some point that their liquor cabinet was getting depleted, but, like everything else, they didn't. But then again, they would have had to have been home more to actually notice.

"You *do* drink, right, Patrick?" Nualla asked, in a worried voice.

I smiled up at her. "Of course, just not normally in public."

I looked back at the shot glass. Once I took one drink, there would be no going back; the evening would take a completely different direction, I just knew it. But was I ready to go down that path?

I looked up at Nualla—into her stunningly beautiful eyes—and didn't really have to think about it after that.

I took a deep breath, and raised my glass up to join theirs. A grin spread across all their faces, and we all downed our shots.

As the shot burned its way down my throat, warming my chest, I nearly choked. "What *is* this?" I asked, looking at the glass.

"Tequila," Nikki answered, grinning.

"*Good* tequila," Shawn amended with a huge grin as he nudged me with his elbow.

I decided it was best not to ask how much "good tequila" cost in a place like this.

A shot or two later, Nualla finally grabbed my hand, and dragged me into the throng of people on the dance floor. People moved against each other, bodies slick with sweat. I was sure there must have been air conditioning running at full-blast, but it really wasn't doing all that much to ease the heat out on the dance floor.

As Nualla began to pulse along with the

music, and I thanked everything holy that I actually *knew* how to dance. She moved with the music hypnotically, and I tried to burn the image in my mind. Because I was sure I was never going to get this lucky again, and I wanted to remember this forever.

Someone brushed up against me and I turned. Apparently Nikki and Shawn had decided to join us out on the dance floor. And as we all danced together, the songs flowing past us like water, I saw something in their movements—their eyes— that told me they were more than "just friends." However, I seriously doubted they had figured that out yet, and that realization brought a grin to lips.

And it was a little comforting to see this other side of them all. The one they didn't show at school. The one that was probably a lot closer to their true selves than anyone else probably ever got to see. Which made me feel strangely honored that they felt they could share at least this small piece of their true selves with me. I had been a silent observer for so long that being invited into their private world was a little overwhelming— overwhelming, but welcome. It was nice to be on the inside for once.

Nualla grabbed my hand, and pulled me a little closer. I nearly froze, but then I released all my fear and just went with it. Letting the music wash over me. Letting it direct my movements. My body moving closer to hers, a cushion of hot air the only thing keeping us from touching. A strange synergy pulling us together. Making us into some strange new creature. And I had to wonder if I would ever feel this complete— this much a part of something—as I did in this moment.

The music went through several changes before Nualla pushed me softly away, and turned her head to Nikki. "Ready, Nikki?"

Nikki smiled broadly as if they were sharing a private joke. "Yep."

"Three...two...one," the girls mouthed with a mischievous, knowing glint to their eyes. And when the music changed, they were standing in the center of the dance floor.

Their hips swiveled, arms thrust, feet stepped in perfect unison. Their bodies pulsing with the music as if made for it. Their precise movements would probably rival any professional dance squad, and put any cheer team to shame. And I couldn't help it as my mouth dropped open.

But even though they moved so perfectly together, I was really only watching one of them. Nikki was hot, and a good dancer in her own right, but she had nothing on Nualla. Nualla moved in time with music as if she was direct- ing a symphony with her body. But it was more than that. Nualla didn't just simply move with the music—she *was* the music. Nualla was song in liquid form; undulating in smooth sensuous movements. She was sex appeal incarnate. And it rolled off her in nearly visible waves, seeming to affect everyone around her. All the guys surrounding the dance floor were staring at her and so were half the women. Entranced with her movements like she was a flame and we were all moths helpless to resist her pull.

A guy, who looked like the love child of Adam Lambert and Freddie Mercury, elbowed me gently, and leaned in. "She's hella hot."

And my protective defenses kicked in. "She's with me."

The guy folded his arms, and looked me up and down, appraisingly. "You're damn lucky. That girl is never here with anyone. She always just seems to be dancing for herself."

"What do you mean?"

He unfolded his arms, and pointed at Nualla. "Look at her eyes. She's looking straight at you. She never looks at anyone when she dances."

"Really?" I replied, looking back at Nualla as she spun, her hair flowing out in a beautiful wave of soft black spirals.

"Yeah...look, she's a little sex rocket. You better be careful, or you might get burned."

"I'll keep that in mind," I said without looking at him, but no answer came. I looked next to me, the guy was gone. I looked back at the girls and was hit full force by Nualla's captivating eyes, which glowed as if illuminated from within.

The girls popped their hips, and dropped to the floor as the song ended. And I just kinda gaped at them as everyone else cheered. Was this how rich people normally lived, or was it just them?

Nualla stood up in one fluid movement, looking at me from beneath her lashes. And everything fell away so there was nothing but her. I swallowed hard. I had never seen anything so sexy and enchanting in my life. *Ever*.

She glided over to me, and reached out a hand to run her finger down my chest. I opened my mouth to say something, but nothing came out. It suddenly felt very warm. *Too* warm.

Nualla pulled me dangerously close, and brought her face to mine. Her lips brushing against my ear as she let out a breath. A breath that was hot and full of temptation. An electric shock ran through my body making my vision sway in and out, and I caught a glimpse of something—something curved near her ear. But as I tried to focus on it, it shimmered farther from my vision.

And that's when I finally realized just how *very* close she was, and that I was touching her. And that if I wanted to, now was probably the best chance I was ever going to get to kiss her. And oh *god,* I wanted to kiss her.

My pulse seemed to be running a fifty yard dash, and it was hard to remember to breathe. I took a deep breath, and swallowed hard.

You can do this.

I leaned in, and Nualla's lips parted ever so slightly like she knew exactly what was about to happen. I was so close. So *very* close. But then I... Well, I completely and utterly lost my nerve. And bolted. Like a total loser.

The Impossible Dream

Friday, January 13th

NUALLA

I THOUGHT PATRICK WAS GOING to kiss me. I *so* wanted him to kiss me. Probably more than I had ever wanted anything. Because there was a sweet, intoxicating danger promised in that kiss. A danger I was longing to embrace with both arms. But he had just left me standing all alone in a sea of people with my heart in my throat.

He had no idea what I was—*who* I was—and yet he had still run.

I watched his form disappearing through the crowd for a moment longer before I turned and walked away. I thought this time it would be different. Apparently I was wrong.

Why do they always run?

"Where's Patrick?" Shawn asked as I dropped down onto the booth seat next to him. The lights dancing over his pale blond hair, making it look like it was on fire.

I shrugged as I picked a shot glass from the tray. "Not sure, he just kinda took off toward the back of the club."

Shawn looked out over the dance floor, and then down at the collection of empty shot glasses. "Maybe he had to throw up."

"*That's* glamorous," I said, rolling my eyes before I tipped the shot down my throat.

"Hey, he *is* human, you know. He can't drink as much as we can. And unless he ate before he ran into you at the mall I'm fairly certain he was doing it on an empty stomach."

I paused before I placed my shot glass back on the tray. He did have a point.

"Maybe you should check on him," I suggested as I picked up the last shot on the tray. Even if it *was* true, the feeling of rejection still felt like a punch to the chest.

"No way in *hell*," Shawn said with a snort as he raised his glass toward mine. "I'm not going to embarrass the frak out of him like that."

"But."

"Nope," Shawn replied shaking his head. "Only way I'm doing that is if we need to leave and he still hasn't come out."

"*Fine,*" I said heavily as I clinked my glass against his.

PATRICK

Y OU SO DID *NOT* JUST **totally do that,"** I groaned under my breath where I sat on the floor of the blessedly cool mens restroom, my back against the wall.

"You just blew your one and only chance with her, you complete and utter fucking idiot!" I admonished myself right as someone shoved open the restroom door.

The guy—a darkly tanned male model type—all but sauntered over to the urinals, humming out of sync with the music that was beating a rhythm through the floor. He unzipped his fly and started to relieve himself before he finally seemed to notice I was there.

"What's your deal—you drink too much?"

"Not enough," I replied for some reason.

"*Hmm...*" the guy replied, looking back at the wall in front of him. "A girl?"

"How'd you guess?" I asked dejectedly.

"Well, my advice—whatever it is that you fucked up, drink some more, it will make it all better."

"*Seriously*?" I asked, looking over at him.

"Naw, but it *will* make you care a whole fucking lot less," the guy said with a snort as he zipped up his fly.

"Oh, *thanks*," I mumbled sarcastically.

"You're welcome," he replied as he turned around. "Oh, and another piece of advice," he said, hooking his thumbs in the front pockets of his jeans. "Don't sit on public restroom floors, they're dirty as fuck."

"I'll keep that in mind," I called after him as he passed the sinks, and pushed the restroom door open.

When I finally found Nualla again, she and Nikki and Shawn were at a cushioned booth table the color of charred wood, doing shots with a few other clubbers.

I snatched up one of the glasses and did a shot with them, slamming it down on the table with a thunk I couldn't hear so much as feel. I probably should have been taking it a bit slower, but I was too pissed at myself to really give that much of a fuck. I picked up the next one as the guy from before—the one who looked like the Adam Lambert-Freddie Mercury love child—poured the next round for everyone.

After I dumped it down my throat I noticed that Shawn was looking at me. "You okay?" he asked me as he picked up his own shot.

"Never better, just a little warm," I flat-out fucking lied, because seriously, who was I kidding?

"Maybe you should—"

"I *know*! I wish I could take off more clothes," Nualla shouted over the music as she tugged on her slashed shirt to illustrate her point. Her cheeks were flushed, and she nearly missed the table when she went to put her empty shot glass down.

Nualla took a wobbly step out of the booth, and all but fell into me. She was apparently more than wasted. Which just made me wonder how many drinks they had had while I was gone?

I wrapped my arm around Nualla to steady her as Nikki laughed so hard she snorted. "I'm sure *he* wouldn't mind, Nualla."

I just coughed as the sudden rush of heat filled my cheeks, because it was the truth. I would have been the biggest liar in the world if I said I hadn't fantasized about what Nualla might have looked like with nothing on.

I looked down and swallowed hard when I realized Nualla's chest was pressed up against my side. Just a thin piece of fabric between me and— I needed a distraction. Oh *god,* did I need one.

I cycled through ideas and tried to ignore how good she felt pressed against me until something reasonably good surfaced.

"What was that about?" I asked, gesturing to the dance floor.

Nualla looked where I was indicating briefly before looking back at me. More of her body pressing against mine. "Oh the dance routine?"

I looked down into her eyes, which was a big mistake, because they had a dreamy, far-away quality to them that stole my breath away. "Yeah," I answered breathlessly.

"Oh, me and Nikki take dance for our PE credits. Why, what do you do?" Nualla answered, her words starting to slur together a bit.

"I just go to the boring ordinary gym. Which is apparently, not *nearly* as useful as what you do," I stated unsteadily, imagining her hot, sweaty body contorting itself into beautiful shapes.

"I'll bet!" Nikki chimed in loudly. "Nualla's been at it like, her whole life. She's like, the most flexible person in our whole class."

"I am! Want to see?" Nualla asked, with a huge grin.

"I—" I was doomed; that's what I was. Either they were fucking with me, or they were smashed beyond all reason. Or *both*.

As I stood there with my mouth hanging open, the music changed and Nualla squealed,

"Oh I *love* this song. Come dance with me."

I looked at her and then the dance floor and then downed another shot for good measure. This turned out to be an incredibly *bad* idea, of course, because when I took a step forward the world began to turn out of kilter.

If you've ever been drunk, you know that there's a point when you've had too much and everything stops making any real sense. You start to feel like you're floating or walking through a dream. Yeah, I had apparently hit *that* point.

Nualla pulled me to the dance floor and slid my hands onto her thrusting, popping, and swaying hips. Her body beneath my hands like a siren's call. Like she was performing a strange, beautiful magic and I was her willing sacrifice. And for the first time since this week started, I began to let myself believe—that I could be with her. That this could really work. That I could just let go and let things happen and everything would be okay. That the outcome of this could be something other than a broken heart so massively damaged that nothing would ever be able to fix it. And there was something dangerously fantastic about it—believing that the impossible really *could* come true.

As we moved together out on the dance floor, I could feel something deep inside of me, screaming that there was danger behind those beautiful eyes. But it would never be able to drown out how badly I wanted to be with her. She had me. I would be hers now and always. And there was something terrifying in knowing that if she asked for it, I would gladly give my life to move heaven and earth to give her anything in the universe.

Nualla looked up at me questioningly. "What?"

"There's something not quite normal about you, isn't there?" I said, my face so very close to hers. The need to press my body against hers was so strong, I was losing the ability to resist it.

"Yeah," she answered, confirming my conclusions.

"Care to enlighten me?" I asked as I looked deep into her eyes.

"Sorry—can't," she answered, shaking her head.

"Why?" I asked, the desperate need to know seeping into the word.

"You'd have to marry me first," she replied in a teasing voice.

"Okay," I answered breathlessly.

I wasn't sure why I had said it. It had just kind of popped out of my mouth, and in the fog of this drunken dream it had begun to make more and more sense.

She stopped dancing, and just stared at me. "*Excuse me*?"

I tried to work through the fog in my head,

but gave up and said the first thing that came to mind. "Were you bluffing again?"

"No..." Nualla admitted very slowly, a smirk spreading across her lips.

"Then let's go," I said as I took a step toward the door, pulling her along, a big dumb grin on my face. I didn't really know why everything seemed incredibly funny when you were drunk, it just did.

"*Now*?" she asked incredulously as she looked over at Nikki and Shawn who were amidst a conversation with some fellow clubbers. All of them laughing so hard they were nearly gasping.

"Sure, why not? What have we got to lose?" I replied, with a shrug.

Nualla stared back at me for a moment before a strange, mischievous light sparked in her eyes. "Okay," she answered slowly, her smile growing broader with every heartbeat.

As we broke out from the club and dashed into the cool night air, I had never felt more alive. We ran down the street toward the future, laughing like idiots. And I couldn't remember the last time I had been this happy—this *free*.

Why in the name of all reason I had said yes, I will never know. Maybe it was because Nualla was beyond tempting, and I was dying to know her secrets. Or that I was angry with my parents for never being there, and I wanted someone to be close to me. Or that I was really, *really* drunk.

But it was probably because, when fate throws you the one thing you have always wanted, you grab hold of it and never let go.

Waking Up in Vegas

Saturday, January 14th

NUALLA

P ARAKALO MAKARA *Aku, Kira, mai Chan*," the boy with the dark eyes whispered before I broke free of the strange dream. I clawed at the bed in the blinding brightness of morning, and stumbled ungracefully toward what I hoped was a bathroom. My head felt like it had made friends with a ton of bricks, and I was beyond thirsty.

I found the sink and splashed cold water onto my face. And that's when I saw it, glittering on my finger. A ring. A really *nice* ring. I took a step back and stared at myself in the mirror. Why the hell was I *naked*?!

I just stared at myself in the mirror for a while in complete shock until something caught my attention. A mark between my hip bone and abdomen.

Is that a hickey?

I inspected it a bit closer. It totally *was* a hickey.

"What the hell!"

"*Ughhh...*" groaned someone's voice from the other room.

I froze. I was in a hotel room—naked—and I wasn't alone. This was bad. This was really, *really* bad.

Oh, gods, Nualla, you really frakked up royally this time.

I edged toward the door of the bathroom and carefully peered out. There was a guy sleeping in the bed.

Oh frak!

I stalked into the room as quietly as I could. And in one swift motion, I snatched a sheet from the floor that had been kicked off the bed in the night and wrapped it over me like a Grecian goddess. Holding my breath, I crept around the bed to stand in front of the still-sleeping guy. I peered closer, and let out a sigh of relief. It was Patrick.

I ran my teeth nervously over my bottom lip; there was no point in putting this off any longer than I needed too. If I was awake and having to deal with this, he should be too. I reached out a tentative hand and poked him with one finger.

Patrick groaned and opened one eye. "*Nualla?*" he asked, my name coming out in a groggy, slurred voice. Then his eyes went wide, and he sat bolt upright. Apparently, the fact that I was wearing a sheet had chiseled its way through his morning fog. He looked at me, looked around the room, and put his head in his hands. "Oh, hell."

I thrust my left hand at him. "Patrick, never mind everything else, what's *this*?"

Patrick spread his fingers to peer at the ring glittering on my finger, and that's when I realized there was a silver band encircling one of his fingers. He dropped his hands, and his eyes went wide. Then he just stared at the ring for a moment before he looked back at me again. "But...I...that was just...a strange dream?"

"Want to try that one again, buddy?" I said flatly.

Patrick pulled the blanket tight to him and leapt out of the bed. Making a mad dash to the lower tier of the hotel suite while I dropped down onto the cushioned bench at the foot of the bed. I put my head in my hand and groaned inwardly. *This isn't happening. This isn't happening. This isn't happening.*

Patrick made a sound and I looked up in time to see him pull a leather folder free from under a pile of random junk on the coffee table. However, from this distance I couldn't see what it was. He looked at it for a moment, his eyes darting back and forth before both his eyebrows shot up.

"Oh, *fuck*!" he cursed as he brought his other hand up to it and the blanket dropped to the ground.

I whipped my eyes away from him lightning fast. "What? What is it?" I said to the floor, a blush creeping across my cheeks. Patrick was also apparently *very* naked.

I heard him walk over, and a second later the bed creaked as he dropped down onto the edge of it. I chanced a look to the side and saw that he had the blanket wrapped around his waist like a towel.

"Here," he said as he handed me the leather folder.

I looked at him questioningly for a moment before I flipped it open and stared at it blankly. It was a certificate. I said nothing for a while; just stared at it in disbelief.

Finally Patrick said, "Nualla, say something."

I jerked my head up quickly to look at him. "We got *married* last night?!"

THIS CAN'T BE HAPPENING

Saturday, January 14th

NUALLA

P ATRICK LOOKED BACK AT ME with a queasy grimace. "Technically, I think we got married
early this morning, since it's like three in
the afternoon."

"*What*?!" I yelped, looking toward the windows of the hotel suite, sure that he must be
wrong. But sure enough, bright afternoon light
was spilling through the large floor-to-ceiling
windows.

I whipped my attention back to him. "How
did this even frakkin' happened?!" I shrieked a
bit hysterically.

Patrick opened his mouth to answer, but was

interrupted by the loud musical ringtone of my phone. We both looked down at the phone that was on the floor between us, then back at each other.

I pulled the sheet a bit tighter to my body and leaned over quickly to pick up my phone before it went to voicemail. "Hello?" I said cautiously, because I had just answered my phone without even checking to see who it was and gods-only-knew what *else* I had done last night.

"Nualla, where the hell *are* you?" Nikki shouted into the phone.

Which was a *really* good question. I stood up and scanned the room, but nothing screamed, *You are here, Nualla, you idiot!*

"I haven't a clue. You?" I admitted as I hugged the sheet tighter.

"We're at the Bellagio," Nikki said with a huff.

"I think we're at the Venetian," Patrick said as he picked something up off the nightstand.

"Apparently we're at the Venetian," I related back to Nikki as I rubbed my throbbing head and thanked the gods it wasn't my dad on the other line.

"How did you get *there*? I thought you two were just going out for air?" Nikki practically yelled into the phone.

"Well we were, but...um...it's a long story," I babbled as I tried to think straight.

"With you, they are *always* long stories," Nikki

said, and I could swear I almost heard her eyes rolling through the phone. "Can you just give me the Twitter version?"

"Look, can I call you back after I find my clothes?"

"Your *what*?!" Nikki shouted on the other end of the phone, and I had to pull it away from my head.

"I'll call you back in five, 'kay?" I said quickly before I hung up the phone.

"I found your clothes," Patrick said apologetically.

Tossing the phone onto the bed, I turned and looked where he was pointing. A few feet away was a trail of clothes that lead from the front door of the suite to the king-sized bed.

"Oh, *frak* me!" I cursed as my hands went automatically to my face and the sheet hit the floor.

Patrick put his hand over his eyes lightning fast, a deep blush spreading across his cheeks.

I rushed over and gathered up my clothes, holding them in front of me as I backed toward the bathroom. Once I had crossed the threshold I threw the clothes down and slammed the door shut. Then I wrenched the door back open, and poked my head out. "Get dressed, we're going downstairs in like, five minutes."

"No complaints here," Patrick said, his hand still covering his eyes.

"Good, because I'm in no mood to hear any," I snapped back before I slammed the bathroom door shut again.

Once alone, I took a few deep breaths to settle my nerves. And then I looked down at my pile of clothes, and noticed something was missing.

Oh for frak's sake!

I open the bathroom door again, and peered out. "Um...Patrick?"

"Yeah?" he answered as he buttoned his jeans. His eyes firmly fixed on his pants. And even with how much of a fucking mess this all was, I couldn't help but notice how sleek and perfectly toned his body was.

I took a deep breath, and asked something I never thought I would ever have to ask. "Have you seen my underwear?"

I paced the sleek marble of the Venetian, my fingers drumming out a nervous rhythm on the stone railing as I willed the person to pick up the phone faster.

What seemed an eternity later a girl who didn't sound much older than me, answered cheerily, "Carrie Ann's Grecian wedding temple. How can I help you to—"

"*Arius Nualla Galathea needs to speak with*

your head priestess right now," I fired off rapidly into the phone in Daemotic.

There was a short pause and then the girl asked, "*Is this a joke?*"

"*No this is not a frakkin' joke! Put her on the gods-damned phone!*"

There was a scuffle of noise, and muffled voices, and then someone new said, "*Arius Nualla, first let Carrie Ann say Carrie Ann is honored Arius Nualla would select Citrina Vona for the location of Arius Nualla's wed—*"

"*Arius Nualla needs Carrie Ann to cancel the license,*" I said firmly, cutting her off.

"*Excuse me?*" Carrie Ann replied, so startled she had reverted to English.

"*This was all a huge mistake and Arius Nualla needs Carrie Ann to revoke the Oath.*"

"I...I can not," the priestess sputtered still in English. "You have spoken the words, you have drunk from the cup."

"You gave us *kekkoshi sadara*?!" I shouted incredulously, finally reverting back to English myself.

"But of course."

I tried not to panic. They had given us wedding cider. But of *course* they had, no Daenarian wedding ceremony would have been complete without it. Which completely explained why I had the hangover of the century and couldn't remember a damn thing about how I had ended up naked in a hotel suite with—

Patrick.

Who was human.

"Oh gods," I breathed, my hand coming up to cover my mouth as the horrible realization of how badly I had fucked up hit me.

"Arius Nualla?" someone called out and I realized I was still on the phone with the priestess.

"Yes?"

"I am very sorry, but even if I *was* willing to revoke your oath, I cannot. The license has already been sent to our embassy and to yours. Under the laws of our people you are now legally bound to Patrick Connolly."

On Second Thought, Make That a Triple

Saturday, January 14th

PATRICK

MY HEAD FELT LIKE A two-ton truck had hit it.

God, just how much had we drunk last night? I groaned inwardly as I looked toward the water. Nualla was still pacing back and forth, waving her hands frantically, and talking into her cell in a language I couldn't understand. Though she was speaking quickly, the words flowed over her lips like a beautiful waterfall. It sounded vaguely Elvish, like maybe it was Gaelic or something. What did Gaelic actually sound like, anyways?

And she seemed upset. I mean *sure,* she'd woken up to find herself married to me. But there was something else. Something she wasn't saying out loud, but I could see it in her eyes. Fear. Something was wrong—*very* wrong.

I mulled over the various possibilities in my head. Maybe she had crazy parents that would disown her or something. Or maybe she had some incurable disease. It could be anything really, and the more I thought about it, the more it gnawed at my insides.

I leaned my head back to stare at the fake sky while rather convincing clouds floated across it. It was like being at Disneyland. A Disneyland for adults. I wasn't sure when, exactly I had gone wrong last night. No, that was a lie, I knew *exactly* when. It was around the time I took that first drink.

This morning had started off less than ideal, and I had absolutely no idea what to say to Nualla. But I was almost one hundred percent certain that saying, *I'm sorry, I didn't mean to marry you; I was drunk and convinced I was dreaming the whole thing up*, wasn't it. However, that also left me back at square one as far as things to say were concerned.

But the truth was that even with how fucked this morning was turning out to be, I couldn't say I wouldn't have done exactly the same thing again, given the choice. Because Nualla Galathea was everything I had ever wanted and more.

I heard the scraping of metal on stone, and looked down just as Shawn was pulling up a chair to sit with me. He leaned back in the chair so that the front feet came off the ground and stared up at the fake sky, sipping his coffee slowly as if he didn't have a care in the world.

After a few more minutes of silence, Shawn finally asked, "So...how was *your* night?"

I stared down at the silver band encircling my left ring finger. "I think me and Nualla got married."

Shawn spit out the coffee, and cursed something in a language I didn't know as his chair slammed back down on the ground. He looked at me, eyes wide. "*Excuse me?*"

I held last night's incriminating evidence in front of him.

Shawn ran his hand back through his hair as he looked down at the wedding band. "Well... *shit.*"

He stared at the band a moment longer before he took another slow sip of coffee. Then he looked at the cup and turned toward the nearest barista. "Um miss, can I get the largest espresso you have with a double shot." She nodded as Shawn started to turn back toward me. Then he paused, his eyes darting quickly to me before they went back to the barista. "On second thought, make that a triple."

"Don't you think you already have enough right there?" I asked him as I eyed his huge coffee cup. Their love of coffee was starting to border on obsessive, but really, was I any less weird?

"It's not for me, it's for *you*," Shawn replied as he turned back to me. "Because you are in for what will quite possibly be the worst hangover of your life."

I just looked at him and let out a bitter self-deprecating laugh, "This is going to get worse?"

"You have no idea," he said with a grimace.

NUALLA

I WAS RUNNING SCARED, DRAGGING Nikki through the Venetian. I was losing it, and somehow I had convinced myself if I kept moving, I wouldn't have to admit this mess was real.

When we reached the gondolas, Nikki pulled me to a stop. "Nualla, wait! What's going on?"

I reached into my book bag and pulled out the leather folder, thrusting it into her hands. "This!"

Nikki looked at it in confusion, but as she flipped it open and began to read her eyes got wider. "Is this some kind of joke?" she asked, looking up.

"I *wish* it was," I answered before I began to pace back and forth in front of her.

"Okay, calm down. Maybe no one will find out, and you can forget the whole thing. We can just go down there and have them shred it. I mean isn't this city's slogan, 'What happens here stays here' or something?"

"No, that won't work," I groaned as I leaned against the railing. "I called the temple and they said it had already been sent to our embassy."

Her mouth dropped open. "Wait, you drunkenly walked into the only Daenarian temple in this whole damn city?" Nikki asked in stunned surprise. "Damn, Nualla, you have skills."

"You are *so* not helping right now, Nikki," I said flatly.

"Okay, well, then you have about, oh, I'd say until maybe Tuesday before that gets filed and everyone finds out. And by 'everyone,' I mean your *dad*."

"I *know*, Nikki. But that's not even the worst part," I said, avoiding her eyes.

"How could this possibly be—wait, you didn't *sleep* with him did you?" Nikki asked in a startled voice.

"Well yes, I mean no, I mean—oh hell, I don't know," I admitted as I sat down on the bottom railing of the bridge and put my head in my hands.

"Well, it's simple really, is he currently rolling on the floor in agonizing pain?" Nikki asked as she stood in front of me.

I looked up. "Well, no."

"Has he complained of his veins feeling like they're on fire?"

"Not that I know of, I mean he didn't *mention* anything anyways."

"Has he complained of any pain at *all*?" Nikki asked, a little exasperated.

"Just his head."

"I'm sure *that's* just a hangover," Nikki said as she rolled her eyes.

"Oh what does it matter anyways? I'm still screwed," I groaned as I put my head back in my hands.

"Well *yeah*, but at least this way we don't have to worry about renting a private plane to transport him home."

"You always look at the bright side, don't you?" I said sarcastically.

"There's plenty of fucked up in this situation, but look, at least you're stuck with someone who's cute, smart, funny, and well, worships the ground you walk on," Nikki pointed out as she ticked off Patrick's attributes on her fingers. "I mean hell, you *could* have accidentally married some jerk like Michael."

"Nikki, *anyone's* better than Michael," I said flatly.

"Well, you do have a point there."

PATRICK

NUALLA CAME AND SAT DOWN at the table with impossible grace. "So the good news is, I'm almost one hundred percent sure we didn't sleep together last night. Well, I mean we slept together, we just didn't 'sleep' together," she babbled nervously.

"And that's a good thing?" I asked, raising an eyebrow. "I mean, why the hell else do you drag a random stranger to Vegas?"

She ran her teeth over her bottom lip, and looked very unsure of herself. And it was in that moment I realized that she might *actually* like me, and I had just basically called her a slut. "Um, well I mean—that didn't come out right did it?"

Nualla cocked her head to one side and smirked at me. "*Yeah*—not exactly. Want to try that again?"

"Yes please," I answered, looking up at her sheepishly.

She nodded as if to say, *well go ahead then* and I looked at the wedding band on my finger. I had been infatuated with Nualla since the very moment I had first seen her. But until this week, she had never seemed to notice I even existed. Somehow she possessed an all-consuming power over me, and I braced myself as I asked the next question. "So...why *did* you drag me to Vegas?"

"Because I wanted to get out of town, and it was the first flight leaving," she answered matter-of-factly.

"No I mean why did you ask *me* to come?" I asked in an unsteady voice as I stared at my coffee.

"*Oh*—because of all the boys in school, I like you the best."

I looked up quickly. Nualla was looking at me, her chin resting on her hand, and her wedding ring glittered in the light. A gentle, tentative smile spreading across her lips. And I just stared at her. I had never thought in a thousand years that I would be here—or for that matter, *any-where* with her—but here she was smiling at me, and I was married to her.

I cleared my throat, and continued on with our conversation. Because I really couldn't just go on staring at her like an idiot. "So...us not sleeping together is a *good* thing?"

"Trust me, in this case it's a good thing," she answered, looking away nervously.

"Can you explain why?"

"I—I can't." She rolled her eyes down to the right, running her teeth over her bottom lip. "It's—complicated."

"*How* complicated?"

"I can't tell you..." she replied, still avoiding my eyes.

"Or what, you'd have to kill me?" I asked jokingly.

Nualla's eyes went wide as she looked quickly up at me. "Um...yeah."

I choked on my coffee. I had been entirely joking, but Nualla's eyes told me she wasn't. "What, is your dad a mob boss or something?"

Nualla had a look on her face like she was trying to teach rocket science to a fish. "*Yeah...*something like that."

I leaned back in my chair, covering my mouth with my hand. *Shit*, just what exactly had I gotten myself into?

Nualla reached out a tentative hand to touch mine, and I looked up. "There's more..." she said uneasily.

"The bad part?" I said, bracing myself for what else life could possibly feel like throwing at me this morning.

"Yeah...turns out we actually *did* get married last night."

I just blinked at her a few times before I finally swallowed hard. "So what do we do now?"

DAEMONS
IN THE
MIST

THE MARKED ONES TRILOGY
· BOOK ONE ·

*Patrick's just woken up with one hell of a hangover...
and a new wife. He may think his wish has just
come true, but will he feel the same when he learns
she's not actually human?*

Secrets and super-tech collide in

DAEMONS IN THE MIST!

ABOUT THE AUTHOR

KAT VANCIL grew up in the heart of Silicon Valley, California where she amused herself by telling stories to anyone around her—her family, her friends, random strangers...cats. Eventually she started writing those stories down instead of hanging out in fake Ikea living rooms and telling them to her friends.

A valiant crusader for diversity, Kat blends geek culture, emerging science, and fantastical creatures to craft her unexpected coming-of-age tales of daemon royalty, super-tech, and shifter deities. Kat still lives in the San Francisco Bay Area with her husband, two very crazy studio cats, and eight overfull bookcases. And when not running amuck in the imaginary worlds within her head, she can usually be found frolicking in general geekiness.

You can find Kat online at KATGIRLSTUDIO.COM email her anytime at KAT@KATGIRLSTUDIO.COM and you can totally geek out with her on Twitter at @KATGIRL_STUDIO about cosplay, books, and other geekery.

Are You On The List?

BE ON THE CUTTING EDGE OF KAT'S NEW RELEASES
WHEN YOU JOIN THE LIST!

Sign up for Kat's VIP readers group, THE LIST and receive an email whenever she releases a new title or is running a cool giveaway or promo. Sign up is easy and comes with a FREE eBook gift!

Visit WWW.KATGIRLSTUDIO.COM/KATS-LIST
to get started

What's Next, Kitty Kat?

If you'd like to see what's in store next for you awesome kitties before it releases, you can visit Kat's COMING SOON page WWW.KATGIRLSTUDIO.COM/CS and catch a glimpse of the covers, and visual inspiration for her upcoming releases.

Acknowledgments

As always there are numerous people I would like to thank, but here are just a few:

My husband and best friend in all the world, for letting me bounce crazy ideas off of him for this book and everything else in the years to come. But mostly, for believing in me even when it was hard for me to believe in myself. My alpha readers and beta readers Scott, Gwyn, Chris and Maureen, for telling me the parts you loved, and the parts you didn't, and the parts that made you laugh out loud. For pointing out plot holes, details I only actually wrote down in my head, and generally making the story the best it could be. My editors Scott Aleric and Maureen, for fixing all my dyslexic mistakes and making this book as shiny and awesome as humanly possible. Madeline, for hanging out in fake Ikea living rooms and letting me tell you all about my stories for hours. I miss you already, and wish you the best of luck in your new venture! The guys of the Self Publishing Podcast, Johnny B. Truant, Sean Platt, and David W. Wright for giving me the idea to even make this novella in the first place.

You guys are more awesome than I could ever express. Keep up the fantastic work gentlemen! My NALitChat and Indelibles teammates and the Twitter community at large for your invaluable information, support and camaraderie; without you all, I don't know how I would be able to work in the studio alone all day. My readers, followers, and fans, for your continued support of my work that let's me live this dream every day. The creators of Scrivener, for creating a writing program that seems especially designed for non-linear writers like me. Without you, my stories would be a horrid mess and take twice as long to write. The creators of Pinterest for creating a way to store my visual ideas and share them with the world. And as always, I am eternally grateful to my parents, Bob and Maureen Dillman for their unwavering support of all the things I do; from dance and theater lessons growing up to putting me through art school. You two are the best parents anyone could have.

—Kat Vancil

Made in the USA
San Bernardino, CA
26 September 2016